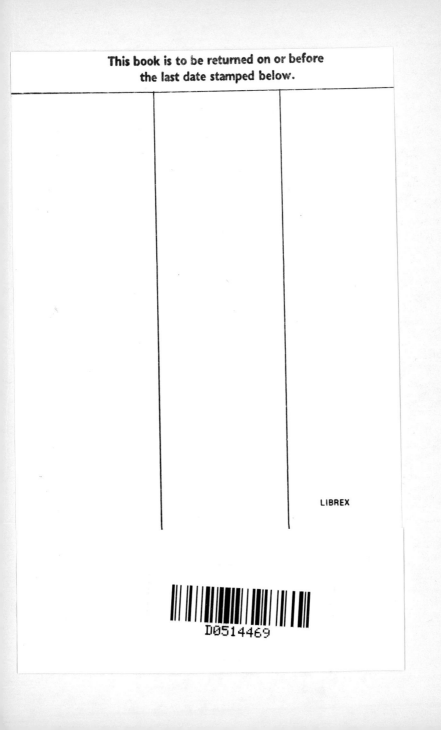

This book is to be returned on or before
the last date stamped below.

LIBREX

D0514469

Also by Martin Beardsley

Sir Gadabout
Sir Gadabout Gets Worse

Sir Gadabout
and the Ghost

Martin Beardsley

illustrated by Tony Ross

A Dolphin
Paperback

For Sophie and Sián

Published in paperback in 1995
by Orion Children's Books
a division of The Orion Publishing Group Ltd
Orion House
5 Upper St Martin's Lane
London WC2H 9EA

First published in Great Britain in 1994
by Orion Children's Books

A catalogue record for this book is available from
the British Library

Typeset by Deltatype Ltd, Ellesmere Port, Cheshire
Printed in Great Britain by Clays Ltd, St Ives plc

ISBN 1 85881 072 8

Contents

1
The Haunted Room

Long, long, ago, when wizards and dragons were as common as warts on a witch's nose, and well before anyone had thought of wearing baseball caps back-to-front, there lived one of the most famous kings of all time: King Arthur.

He was a wise and fair king, and he was married to the beautiful and resourceful Guinevere. So great was her beauty that if she were to drop her handkerchief, knights who were normally very sensible would fight for the honour of picking it up, no matter how many times she had blown her nose on it. She was also a dab hand when it came to making and fixing things. King Arthur and Queen Guinevere never had to resort to the *Yellow Pages* when something went wrong, mainly because the telephone hadn't been invented, but also because they didn't *need* to send for outside help. Guinevere had only recently put

the finishing touches to an ambitious and elaborate guttering and drainage system around the mighty walls of the castle.

The castle was called Camelot, a towering fortress hidden within eerie mists. It was so hard to find that map-makers tended to show it in several different places just to be on the safe side. Inside Camelot were the famous Knights of the Round Table, the best knights in the land all gathered together to protect the weak and save those in distress.

Actually, it is a small fib to say that *all* of the Knights of the Round Table were the best in the land. In fact, ninety-nine out of the one hundred knights seated at the Round Table on this particular day were the best in the land. They were reporting back to King Arthur on the heroic and chivalrous deeds they had performed during the week. Sir Bors told how he had emerged scarred and bruised but triumphant after fighting off ten villains who were chalking rude words on the walls of the

9

castle. Sir Gawain had amicably settled a heated dispute about the weather between two farmers.

But there was one knight who could only mumble, "Well, your Majesty, it's been rather a quiet week . . ."

"Again?"

"I'm afraid so – but I did fish a poor drowning fly out of my cup of tea this morning!" Thus spoke Sir Gadabout, the Worst Knight in the World.

"Was it all right?" asked the King, trying hard to sound interested.

"Yes, your Majesty," replied Sir Gadabout. "Surprisingly, it tasted fine."

"I meant the fly."

"Oh, well, I, er, accidentally put my cup down on top of it. It got a bit squashed," Sir Gadabout admitted.

"I'm sure you did your best," said the King in a kindly voice, knowing that despite his faults – and there were many of them – Sir Gadabout's heart was in the right place.

Then it was Sir Lancelot's turn to report to the King. In contrast to Sir Gadabout, Sir Lancelot was the Greatest Knight Who Ever Lived, but he was a bit full of himself.

"On Monday morning, I did battle with a dragon which was trying to destroy the

village of Runforit – at least that's what I think
they called it. The dragon breathed scorching
flames and its skin was as tough as steel. When
my sword broke I had to fight it with my bare
hands. I noticed that it was vulnerable to a
left-hook, and managed to knock it out with a
perfectly-timed blow to the jaw. Then, on
Monday afternoon, I found myself confronted by an entire army of nomadic
warriors, intent on conquering your lands,
your Majesty . . ."

And so it went on – and on, and on . . . Sir
Gadabout's eyes began to close, and his head
nodded forward. Soon his chin was resting on
his chest, and he was emitting a sound which

he called "deep breathing whilst concentrating". Others described it as "snoring".

As darkness fell, more and more knights became restless. It wasn't that they were afraid of the dark – but of what darkness might bring. The Round Table room was reputed to be haunted. Even those who claimed not to believe in ghosts began to fidget as they noticed the sun sinking slowly below the level of the windows. Those who had been unfortunate enough to encounter the spook were hovering on the edge of their seats, desperate for the meeting to end. So many of them had had their hair turned white trying to conquer the ghost that Cedric, the castle herbalist, was doing a roaring trade in hair-dye. Sir Lancelot himself had once declared he was going to kick the ghost out for good, but soon afterwards he had been seen running out of the Round Table room saying he'd forgotten to put a note out for the milkman.

The great knights were fearless when it came to anything you could stick your sword into, but things that walked through walls and went bump in the night left them just a tad nervous . . .

By the time Sir Lancelot had got on to Wednesday afternoon in his account, the room was becoming gloomier, and dark shadows swallowed up the furthest corners and edged their way towards the Round Table. Sir Kay asked to be excused to go to the toilet and never came back. Sir Brian the Bold produced from his pockets an assortment of lucky charms, crosses, and garlic, which he arranged on the table in front of him. A sudden loud bump almost made the knights jump out of their armour – but it was only Sir Gadabout slumping forward and banging his head on the table, sound asleep. Sir Lancelot, noticing for the first time that someone was finding his tales less than enthralling, paused indignantly, then pressed relentlessly on to Wednesday evening and his duel with the Black Knight of Devil Rock.

While Sir Lancelot was drawing breath between Wednesday night and Thursday morning, King Arthur saw his chance and jumped in.

"I think," he said hastily, "that I must reluctantly call an end to this meeting. I, er, have got to see a very important person."

The very important person was Guinevere, but since she was the Queen, and undoubtedly a very important person, he did not think he could be accused of lying. By now, it was getting so dark that the knights

could hardly see each other across the Round Table, and they were desperate to get out.

There was a loud scraping of chairs and thunder of footsteps as, taking their cue from the King, they thankfully escaped from whatever the darkness might bring. All of them except one . . .

When Sir Latchlock, the Keeper of the Privy Keys, had hastily locked the door and his echoing footsteps slowly faded away, Sir Gadabout was left on the other side to spend the whole night in the dreaded, spine-tingling Round Table room . . .

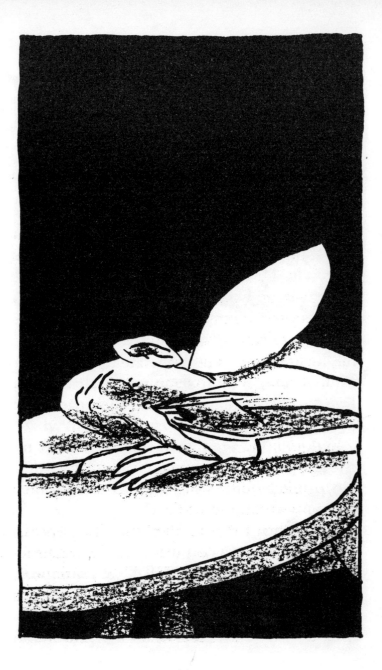

2
A Ghostly Encounter

Blissfully unaware of his predicament, Sir Gadabout slumbered on, his head resting on the table. He was very thin and of no more than average height, but he did have quite a large hooter, and the sound of his snoring was famed and feared throughout Camelot. As he fell into a deeper and deeper sleep, the enormous Round Table began to vibrate noisily, and then started to move, slowly but surely, across the room.

Before long, the table had travelled far enough for Sir Gadabout's head to slip off it. He tumbled out of his chair with a thud, then suddenly sprang to his feet.

"And then I rescued the beautiful princess from drowning in my tea . . ." he began in rather a fuddled voice. "Oh," he continued, peering into the darkness and sounding even more confused. "I can't see a thing! Wait a minute . . ." He looked up and saw the moon

through a window. "I can see when I look up, but I go completely blind when I look down."

After a couple of minutes, his eyes became accustomed to the dark, and with the aid of a little bit of moonlight which was streaming through the window, he finally worked out what had happened. Groping his way over to the door, he discovered that it was firmly locked. The windows were far too high to reach, and anyway the Round Table room was at the very top of Camelot's highest tower. It was so isolated that there was little point in knocking or shouting.

Just when he was thinking that things couldn't get worse, Sir Gadabout remembered the creepy reputation of this part of the castle, and he came over rather faint. He leaned for support on the Round Table, shaking so much that it actually rattled back into its original position.

That was when he discovered that his snoring had not only moved the Round Table . . . it had roused *something* which had been lurking in the darkest corners of the tower. Out of the gloom, a low, angry moan could be heard. It grew louder and louder until it seemed to shake the very walls. The knight tried to make himself believe that it was Sir Latchlock come to let him out.

"Ah, I'm glad you came," said Sir Gadabout. His voice sounded like a mouse's squeak. The room suddenly felt chilly, sending a shiver down his spine.

"GLAD?" bellowed the voice, and with it came a blast of cold air which made icicles appear on Sir Gadabout's moustache. His trembling caused them to play a timorous little tune.

"I – er – didn't mean to stay here. I fell asleep."

"That's *nothing*," exclaimed the voice. "I died of a broken heart!"

"It may be nothing to you," said Sir Gadabout, "but I had to sit listening to Sir Lance – Did you say *died*?"

Suddenly, the glowing figure of a knight emerged from the solid wall opposite Sir Gadabout and floated towards him.

The brave knight let out a shriek which no human could hear, but which started dogs howling from Acton to Addis Ababa. He ran the length of the room, sparks flying from his knocking knees, and when he got to the wall he carried on running until he reached the

ceiling. Grabbing for the nearest window, he missed and plummeted to the floor, a dithering, gibbering pile of arms, legs and rattling armour.

"Oh, it's *you*. What a pathetic sight," groaned the ghost, who cut a fine figure with his broad shoulders and barrel chest (except that you could see through him). "Sometimes it hardly seems worth the effort," he sighed. "Pull yourself together, man. I died ages ago; I'm feeling much better now. It would make a nice change to meet someone man enough to listen to my tale. It's not as if there's anything unusual about me."

"B–but there is," stammered a voice from the floor. "You walk through walls!"

"You seem to run *up* them," accused the ghost.

Sir Gadabout clambered shakily to his feet, his eyes as wide as saucers, and his teeth chattering like a demented woodpecker.

"I've been watching you," said the ghost. "The chair you sit in used to belong to me."

"Y–you c–can have it b–back," said Sir Gadabout, prepared to offer the ghost more or less anything else if only it would go away.

"It's no good to me now, silly man. I'd only fall through it."

"Then w-what do you w-want?" Sir Gadabout begged. "I could get the blacksmith to make you a nice set of chains to rattle, or –"

"No, no," barked the apparition. "I'm not *that* sort of ghost. It's the bally rattlers and shriekers who give haunting a bad name. Now, my man, stand up straight like a real knight and listen to what I have to say."

Sir Gadabout jumped to attention. "Er, I'm listening," he said. He didn't really have any choice.

"I am – or was – Sir Henry Hirsute, as good

and brave a knight as ever there was," said Sir Henry proudly, twiddling the ends of his magnificent handlebar moustache. He had a long, neatly trimmed beard to match. "Why, I once defeated Sir Lancelot!"

Sir Gadabout was impressed. "In a joust?"

"No, at dominoes – but the cad made me promise never to tell anyone."

"But why do you haunt this room?" asked Sir Gadabout.

"A good knight never deserts his post," replied the ghost proudly. "Many years ago I

was accused of stealing a tin of pilchards from the Camelot kitchens."

"Did you say a tin of pilchards?"

"Yes, and please don't interrupt me again. I've waited ten years to tell this story. I didn't do it of course – no Knight of the Round Table would steal. But I have to admit all the evidence was against me. A man of my description – claiming to be me, in fact – did the deed. He made off with the pilchards, bold as brass. The only honourable thing to do was leave Camelot to save King Arthur

from embarrassment. However, I was so unhappy – though I'm not normally given to soppiness, you understand – that I died of a broken heart, right here, in the middle of one of Sir Lancelot's long speeches. Then I found myself stuck here, destined to haunt the Round Table room until my innocence can be proved."

"Must you stay here *forever*?" asked Sir Gadabout.

"Yes," Sir Henry replied, putting on a brave face. "Unless, that is, the person who really did steal the pilchards is brought to justice. Then I would be set free."

"Tell me who it was," said Sir Gadabout boldly, determined to help a fellow knight, ghost or otherwise, in distress. "I, Sir Gadabout, shall bring him to account."

Sir Henry looked Sir Gadabout up and down and shook his head. "It all happened ten years ago, and I fear it is much too late. All I know is that on the day the pilchards went missing, a travelling knife-sharpener was at work in the kitchens. He had never been to Camelot before, nor, for all I know, has he been seen since . . ."

"Oh dear," said Sir Gadabout, dismayed. "It all sounds very fishy." Sir Henry gave him a stern look and his shimmering form turned from silvery grey to angry red.

"Er . . . that is . . ." spluttered Sir Gadabout, "when I said 'fishy' I didn't mean . . . well, I meant . . ."

"Hmm, no offence taken," said the ghost, paling once more to silvery grey.

"I intend to get to the bottom of this," declared Sir Gadabout, "and release you from your torment!"

"Good man!" replied Sir Henry. He didn't look too hopeful about his prospects, but he bade Sir Gadabout farewell; vanished through the wall at a brisk march and left the knight to get some sleep.

3
Merlin's Crystal Ball

The following morning, after Sir Gadabout had been released from the Round Table room, his faithful squire, Herbert, came hurrying to find him. He had heard rumours: *"Sir Gadabout has been accidentally locked in the haunted room all night . . . the ghost has stolen Sir Gadabout's pilchards . . . his hair has turned white and his trousers have fallen down . . ."* Some of the rumours may have become a little distorted in all the excitement, and Herbert was keen to discover if his master was safe and well.

"Sire, are you all right?" asked Herbert, a short but sturdy lad with ham-like fists which had served Sir Gadabout well in the past.

"Of course I'm all right," Sir Gadabout replied. He was eating his breakfast with the other knights. Herbert overheard more whispered rumours: *". . . he tried to walk through a wall and knocked himself out . . . he thinks he's the ghost of a tin of pilchards . . ."*

"We've got work to do today," said Sir Gadabout. "It's all to do with pilchards."

Herbert was dismayed. "Of course, sire – but perhaps you'd like a nice lie-down first?"

"I must admit, I am rather tired. But there's no time. We have a lot of travelling to do."

"Why?" Herbert was almost afraid to ask.

"Herbert, I saw the ghost last night," Sir Gadabout began.

"Oh, dear," said Herbert, expecting to

hear about the spooky pilchards at any moment.

"None other than the ghost of Sir Henry Hirsute," Sir Gadabout went on.

"I've heard stories about him," said Herbert. "He was a crooked knight, wasn't he?"

"Most certainly not! He was accused of stealing a tin of pilchards, but he was completely innocent." Sir Gadabout went on to tell Herbert about the knife-sharpener. "He is the key to the whole thing, I am certain.

Therefore, I intend to visit all the knife-sharpeners in the land in order to find out which one visited Camelot when the pilchards were stolen. If he didn't steal them, he may know who did."

Herbert's heart sank. There were several knife-sharpeners in most towns in the land; he and Sir Gadabout would almost certainly die of old age before they had visited half of them. He had to think quickly – there must be a better way of doing things.

"What if we visited Merlin?" he suggested. Merlin was King Arthur's powerful and mysterious wizard.

"He's never been a knife-sharpener as far as I know . . ." said Sir Gadabout.

"No, sire," replied Herbert patiently, "but he may be able to give us some clues as to where to start looking."

Sir Gadabout leapt to his feet. "Splendid idea!" he cried, throwing his spoon down rather too enthusiastically; there was a splash, and both he and Herbert found themselves covered in milk and cornflakes.

"*Poor old Gads*," Herbert heard someone whisper. "*Thinks Herbert's a tin of pilchards, you know . . .*"

Sir Gadabout and Herbert hurried across Camelot's great drawbridge and made their

way to Merlin's cottage, deep in Willow Wood. When they arrived at the garden gate they saw a noticeboard. Sir Gadabout had grown used to such signs, which warned visitors about the wizard's imaginative but hopeless guard-turtle, Dr McPherson.

This latest sign, however, was even more puzzling than usual. It was like a "House For Sale" sign: a wooden board on the end of a long stick, which was stuck into a little mound of earth by the gate. Herbert saw it as he was opening the gate for his master, and

remarked, "That's odd – 'BEWARE OF THIS SIGN'."

Sir Gadabout tapped the board experimentally with his knuckles, and Herbert winced, expecting it to explode, or perhaps electrocute his master, but nothing happened.

"Beware of This Sign – what nonsense!" snorted Sir Gadabout. Having spent the night in a haunted room, he was feeling much braver than usual. But if he had looked down, he would have seen the 'mound of earth' move . . .

It was Herbert who spotted the danger first. "Look out, sire!" he cried, just as the turtle burst from his hiding place, brandishing the sign like a baseball bat. Knight and squire dashed down the path towards the cottage, Dr McPherson hard on their heels. With a cry of "BANZAI!" the board came swishing this way and that, just missing their heads. Not to be defeated, the turtle steadied himself, and with a blood-curdling, "YAH!", let fly the sign like a javelin. Sir Gadabout and Herbert threw themselves to the ground. At that moment, the cottage door opened and out stepped Sidney Smith, Merlin's clever but short-tempered, sarcastic ginger cat.

"What's all this n –" he began. WHAM! The sign caught him smack between his green eyes and sent him flying backwards head-over-heels . . . or possibly heels-over-head . . . Hauling himself unsteadily to his feet, he spotted Sir Gadabout and Herbert. "Ah, my dear friends," he said. "Do come in. Merlin will be absolutely delighted to see you!"

This was *most* unlike Sidney Smith. "Do you think he's gone a bit. . . ?" began Sir Gadabout.

"Yes," Herbert replied. "But don't say anything – I can just about stand him this way."

They were escorted into the cottage, where Merlin was busy writing in a massive, dusty book. Long, untidy grey hair hid his face, which was pressed close to the page. Sidney Smith slipped under the table and brushed his portly body against Merlin's legs, purring.

"What on *earth* . . ." began the wizard. Then he looked up, and his piercing blue eyes fell upon Sir Gadabout and Herbert. "I thought I said I was *not* to be disturbed?"

"Oh, but master," said the cat, "these are our delightful friends, the brave Sir Gadabout and the witty, intelligent Herbert!"

Herbert frowned and scratched his head. He and Sidney Smith were usually at each other's throats, and he began to wonder if he was having his leg pulled. But Merlin, being the great wizard that he was, and noticing the bump on his cat's head, quickly assessed the situation. Tweaking Sidney Smith's ears, he picked him up and turned him round three times, then tugged his tail with a cry of, "*SHAZZAM!*"

Sidney Smith blinked and eyed Sir Gadabout disdainfully. "Why, it's the bungling bean-brain from Camelot and his pint-sized oaf! Scram! Can't you see my master's busy?"

Herbert hated rude remarks about his size or his master's intelligence, and was just about to grab the cat by the scruff of its neck when Merlin said wearily, "Now they're here, they might as well tell me what they want."

Sir Gadabout once more went through his story about Sir Henry Hirsute and the pilchards.

"Bah!" said Merlin, "I could have got rid of the ghost ages ago if King Arthur didn't insist on keeping the place locked up every night.

But if, as you say, it has something to do with a knife-sharpener whom you need to trace, I may be able to help you."

Getting up from the table, he made his way across the cluttered, cobwebby room, and took a wooden box from a chest of drawers. Inside was a crystal ball which he placed on the table. The wizard sat down and stared into it. After a few seconds a swirling golden mist appeared inside the ball, and he began to speak in a faraway voice.

"Long ago . . . in the kitchens of Camelot . . .

*Sir Henry Hirsute . . . knocks cook out of way
. . . steals pilchards . . ."*

"No!" complained Sir Gadabout. But it is
very unwise to disturb a wizard when he is
gazing into a crystal ball. There was a sharp
crackle, and a bolt of silver-blue lightning
snaked from the ball and struck Sir Gadabout
on the helmet, travelling down his armour
and making the armour plating on his feet
explode. "Ooh! Owww!" he yelled, hopping
from one foot to the other, his socks in tatters
and plumes of acrid smoke rising from his
toes.

"Never – NEVER do that again!" Merlin
shouted.

"I'm very sorry," Sir Gadabout apolo-
gised. "But I *know* Sir Henry told me the
truth. Could you try looking back a little
earlier, before he came into the kitchen?"

After giving the knight the sternest of
looks, Merlin went back to his crystal ball. "*I
see a man outside the kitchen – not Sir Henry. He
has red hair and no beard . . . has bag . . . takes
out armour . . . false beard and moustache . . .
goes into kitchen . . . knocks cook out of
way . . .*"

"That's it!" Sir Gadabout exclaimed glee-
fully. This time he didn't even see the bolt of
silver-blue lightning which blew his helmet

off and completely melted his armour so that
he was left staggering around Merlin's room
clad only in his new *Y-Worry?* Y-front under-
pants. (They had openings at both the back
and the front in case, as Sir Gadabout was
prone to do, he accidentally put them on the
wrong way round.)

Merlin continued gazing into the ball, but
because of the disturbances the picture was

fading. "*He leaves on a fast horse . . . rides many miles . . . I see a town called Hope's End . . .*"

The golden cloud inside the ball melted away.

"I must travel to Hope's End forthwith!" declared Sir Gadabout.

"Then you must take Sidney Smith," said Merlin. "You will need his . . ." he was going to say "brains", but decided that that would be too unkind. "You may need his cunning. Sidney?"

But the cat had already made himself scarce.

"Hmm," mused the wizard. "Well, you'll have to manage without Sidney's help. All I can tell you is that there is something very fishy at the bottom of all this."

Sir Gadabout and Herbert laughed politely.

But Merlin wasn't joking. "No, no. I mean *real* fish. I sense this whole thing is to do with fish – lots and lots of fish. Some people collect shells, some collect teapots. This person has a fishy sort of collection."

There was a sudden frantic scraping, scuffling and grunting behind one of Merlin's many bookcases, and a cobwebby Sidney Smith appeared.

"Perhaps I might be of assistance?" he offered. A very small, hungry dribble appeared at the corner of his mouth, and he wiped it away with his paw.

And so it was that Sir Gadabout, Herbert and Sidney Smith commenced their quest to restore the honour of Sir Henry Hirsute.

4

The Journey to Hope's End

The three companions set off for the town of Hope's End the very same day. Sir Gadabout was riding Pegasus, his willing and wheezy old horse, whose legs weren't what they used to be. Herbert was on his pony, with Sidney Smith riding in one of the saddlebags, dozing most of the time and dreaming of fish, but occasionally popping his head out to make a stinging remark about the bumpiness of the ride or to point out that they were going the wrong way.

Sir Gadabout had devised what he believed to be an ingenious plan. He had decided to tell people that they were looking for a first-class knife-sharpener. Since they were from Camelot, they would really prefer one with experience of working in castles – like Camelot, for example. Herbert thought this was a marvellous idea, while Sidney Smith was of the opinion that it was utter hogwash.

It had not occurred to Sir Gadabout that
their man had probably only pretended to be a
knife-sharpener in order to avoid detection.
There were other things which had not occurred to Sir Gadabout either, as he discovered
when they joined a traveller and asked him the
best way to Hope's End. It turned out that he
was making his way back there after a visit to
a cousin in a nearby village.

"And what takes you to Hope's End, my
friend?" asked the stranger.

46

"Ah! I am Sir Gadabout, a Knight of the Round Table, and I have heard that I can find one of the best knife-sharpeners in the land there – one with castle experience!"

"You're travelling all the way from Camelot just to have some knives sharpened?" asked the puzzled man.

Sidney Smith tittered.

"I don't mind a short journey to find a master craftsman, especially one with Camelot-type experience," replied Sir Gadabout, a little offended that his explanation had not been accepted without question.

"You must have a lot of knives to make it worth your while to travel this far," the stranger pointed out.

Sidney Smith's sniggering grew louder.

Sir Gadabout had not thought of that. He only had one knife – a dagger in a sheath fastened to Pegasus' saddle. He drew it out, and as he did so his finger brushed the edge of the blade. "Oww!" he cried, hurriedly hiding his bleeding finger behind his back.

Sidney Smith laughed till the tears streamed down his ginger cheeks. Herbert roughly pushed the cat's head deep into the saddlebag.

"*That* knife needs sharpening?" asked the man incredulously.

"Oh, it's quite blunt now compared with how it used to be," replied Sir Gadabout, looking rather pale. The sight of blood – especially his own – made him feel faint.

The stranger told them the best way to Hope's End and bade them farewell, nervously backing away from them as he spoke, and keeping a wary eye on Sir Gadabout. He rode off, but turned back on hearing another "Oww!" from Sir Gadabout, who had cut his arm and his other hand while replacing the

knife in its sheath.

"Brilliant!" chortled an almost hysterical feline voice from within Herbert's saddlebag.

The upshot of this encounter was that by the time Sir Gadabout, Herbert and Sidney Smith arrived at Hope's End, the story had already reached the town that a lunatic knight from Camelot was on his way, waving razor-sharp knives about. Their arrival was observed by a group of gawping people, for many in Hope's End had never seen a Knight of the Round Table before, and without

doubt, none had seen one quite like Sir
Gadabout. A frail-looking old lady left the
gathering and approached them.

"Hello, my dears," she said. She wore a
blue-checked shawl and had long white hair.
Herbert's sharp eyes noted that she had red
eyebrows. "You'll be needing a room for the
night, I dare say?"

"Yes, madam," replied Sir Gadabout.
"Perhaps you might know of a comfortable
inn?"

"No need, young man. I take people in,

and it just so happens that my rooms are free at the moment. You would be most welcome!"

Sir Gadabout was delighted, and they accompanied the old lady home to a pleasant little house with a thatched roof.

She showed them to their room.

"What a friendly place Hope's End is," said Sir Gadabout after she had left them. "And how lucky we were to come across succh a charming lady."

"I'm not so sure . . ." said Sidney Smith.

"Trust you to be a misery," Herbert scolded him.

"No," protested the cat. "It's just that she –" He was interrupted by a knock at the door. It was the old lady with their evening meal. She was carrying a vast tray, so laden with food they could hardly believe that such a small and elderly person could lift it. Putting it down on the table, she began to show them various delicious dishes covered with dome-shaped lids to keep them warm. "And this," she finished, tapping another lid, "is my special pudding – Pineapple Fizz!"

They thanked her warmly, and she left them to eat their meal.

"What's that noise?" asked Sir Gadabout in between mouthfuls of potato.

"It seems to be the special pudding, sire," replied Herbert. They all leaned closer to the dome-shaped lid, and discovered that the Pineapple Fizz was indeed fizzing underneath.

"What fun!" said Sir Gadabout.

"I don't think so," said Sidney Smith in alarm. He picked the pudding up and made as if to lift the lid. "I think it's –"

"Hey!" said Sir Gadabout, trying to wrestle it from the cat. "Leave it alone till we've finished the first course."

"But I think it's –"

But Sir Gadabout had prised the dish away from the cat. The fizzing sound was even louder by now, and he couldn't resist taking a tiny peek under the lid. He quickly slammed the lid shut again and turned to Herbert.

"It's a b– b–" he stammered.

"A bun?" asked Herbert.

"No, a b– b–"

"Banana Split?"

"No! It's a b– b–" The fizzing grew louder still, and even as the knight was in the act of

throwing the Pineapple Fizz out of the window, there was a flash and an ear-splitting bang, and the room was filled with choking black smoke. But Sir Gadabout had not thrown the Pineapple Fizz away quickly enough. His face was completely blackened, and only one smouldering hair remained on the top of his head.

"A b– bomb . . ." he said finally in a rather strange voice, and as he spoke a little cloud of black smoke came puffing out of his mouth.

"The old lady!" cried Sidney Smith,

bounding out of the door.

"But she wouldn't . . ." protested Herbert, running after him.

"Is it Wednesday, or January?" a dazed Sir Gadabout enquired of a broom standing in the corner.

They searched the house frantically, but could find no trace of the little old lady. Just as they were leaving, they heard the sound of banging in the kitchen. Rushing to investigate, they found that it was coming from a cupboard under the sink. Sir Gadabout, who

had now recovered whatever wits he had, opened the door. Inside was a little old lady with white hair, tied up and gagged.

"Why, you . . ." began Herbert menacingly.

"Wait," said Sidney Smith. "We've been tricked. This is the *real* old lady. The one we met must have been in disguise. And remember, the person who stole the pilchards managed to disguise himself as Sir Henry Hirsute!"

"Er, just as I thought," said Sir Gadabout, trying to sound wise but failing. He was

totally baffled. "I can hear more banging!" he suddenly exclaimed, as they untied the old lady. "Someone else has been kidnapped!"

"I think it's someone at the door, sire," said Herbert.

"Of course it is," said Sir Gadabout. "Well, open it!"

Herbert opened the door and was confronted by a stoutly built man with a leathery face and a broken nose. He was dressed in fine clothes, and carried a thick, silver-tipped stick.

"I come from Baron Godfrey," announced

the visitor importantly.

"Who's he when he's at home?" asked Herbert, unimpressed.

"He owns all the land hereabouts. I'm his steward, and I'm responsible," he said, tapping the stick sharply against the palm of his hand, "for law and order."

Herbert and Sir Gadabout were suitably impressed, but clever Sidney Smith had spotted a tuft of red hair peeping from underneath the steward's blue silk cap, and smiled quietly to himself.

"I'm glad you came," said the little old lady. "You see, I was just having my elevenses – I like to have digestive biscuits with my tea, although I don't dip them in, because I think that's rather –"

"And that," interrupted the steward impatiently, "is when he pushed you into the cupboard. Disgraceful! The Baron shall hear of this."

Herbert was trying to work out how the steward could have known this, while Sir Gadabout was marvelling at the man's detective skills. But Sidney Smith knew better, and remained silent.

"And then," added Sir Gadabout helpfully, "she – I mean he, in disguise – gave us a Pineapple Fizz. I wouldn't recommend

Pineapple Fizz because –"

"Baron Godfrey will be *outraged* to hear that a bomb was set off without his permission!"

"Er I suppose so," agreed Sir Gadabout, with the wind taken out of his sails somewhat.

"And do we know who was responsible for these dastardly deeds?" asked the steward, his stick quivering impatiently.

Sir Gadabout put his hand up, hoping to be allowed to explain a theory he had been developing. But this was all the steward needed.

"You confess!" he cried, pointing his stick at Sir Gadabout.

"It wasn't him!" yelled Herbert.

"*Might* have been," said Sidney Smith wickedly. And feeling sure he knew who the steward really was, he did a little fishing of his own. "He might have been after the old lady's rare tinned halibut to add to his collection back at Camelot."

The steward's imperious expression changed. "I didn't know you could get halibut in a tin . . ." there was a slight tremor in his voice.

"You can't in this country. He had to travel all the way to Sardinia. It was worth it, to put

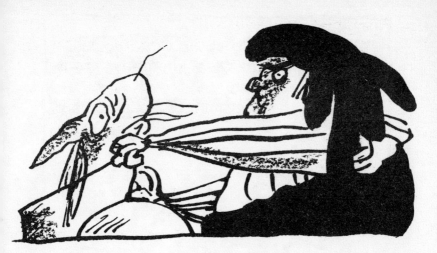

it alongside his turbot, hake and stickleback –
things like that."

"All in tins?" cried the steward, now
almost beside himself with agitation.

"Of course," replied Sidney Smith as if it
were the most natural thing in the world.

"Right," commanded the steward, grabbing Sir Gadabout by the scruff of the neck.
"You're going away for a very long time
indeed!" and he frog-marched the unfortunate knight to the town's jail.

"What on earth was all that about?" asked
Herbert angrily. "We're in a proper pickle
now."

"He was going to lock the old duffer up
anyway," replied Sidney Smith. "I've just
given us a chance to get our own back."

5

Rufus Redhead, Master of Disguise

As soon as they had made sure that the real old lady had quite recovered, Herbert and Sidney Smith hurried to the jail. Sir Gadabout was not locked up but sitting on the ground outside with his hands and feet fastened in the stocks. A little gang of boys was throwing rotten tomatoes and some even worse things at him.

"Let me out!" spluttered Sir Gadabout, spitting out tomato pips. "He's gone to fetch the hangman!"

"Don't worry, fishface," said Sidney Smith. "I think you'll find the steward has scarpered."

Their conversation was interrupted by the sound of frantic banging coming from inside the jail. Herbert quickly went over and opened the door. Out fell the steward. He was tightly bound with strong rope and had a gag over his mouth.

"*That's* the one who tied me up!" accused the steward as soon as Herbert had removed the gag from his mouth. He was pointing at Sir Gadabout.

"No!" protested Sir Gadabout from the stocks, as a mouldy peanut whizzed into his mouth. "It wasn't me!"

"I don't think he tied himself up, sire . . ." Herbert said respectfully.

"Er . . ." said Sir Gadabout, scratching his head in bewilderment.

"Could it be," Sidney Smith suggested just a trifle smugly, "that the steward who brought you here – and who had a *wee* tuft of red hair – locked you in the stocks, then disguised himself as you . . ."

"Then," interrupted Herbert, "he must have been disguised as Sir Gadabout when he tied the real steward up."

"Ummm, if he was dressed as me," pondered Sir Gadabout, "and I was dressed as . . . no, hang on – if he locked me up, then I was dressed as . . ."

"I think you'll find *this* explains everything," said Sidney Smith. He had been investigating some 'Wanted' posters pinned to the door of the jail:

WANTED
RUFUS REDHEAD
MASTER OF DISGUISE
Rufus Redhead will go to any lengths
to gather the finest collection of tinned fish
in the world. Is wanted on countless
charges of theft and deception.

DESCRIPTION
Tall or short, fat or thin, male or female.

Underneath there was an artist's impression of a tall, short, fat, thin man or woman wearing a wig showing a tiny tuft of red hair peeping out underneath.

"He knew we were on to him," explained Sidney Smith, "thanks to the Worst Knight in the Universe and his Master Plan. The whole town knew who we were and why we were coming, and it wouldn't have taken long to put two and two together. First he tried to bump us off, then when I told him about Gads's collection of tinned fish, he couldn't resist going after that."

"Perhaps I haven't recovered from my bump on the head," said Sir Gadabout, rather overwhelmed by the turn of events. "I didn't even know I *had* a collection of tinned fish."

"You haven't," said Sidney Smith, rolling his eyes. "But *he* doesn't know that. I bet you he's off to Camelot to try and get his hands on it. Little does he know he's played nicely into my paws."

"But he might do *anything* once he gets there – and he's disguised as Sir Gadabout!" said Herbert fearfully. "Look what happened to Sir Henry Hirsute!"

"Well," replied Sidney Smith, wearing a crooked smile, "there is a risk that, if we don't get back quickly enough, or if we're not clever enough when we get there, Gads will end up having his head chopped off . . ."

Sir Gadabout turned pale and made a noise like a kitten when someone treads on its tail. "This is a fine kettle of fish," he groaned.

"Don't worry! We won't let him slip out of the net," declared Sidney Smith with a wink.

6
Sidney Smith's Plan

Sir Gadabout, Herbert and Sidney Smith headed back to Camelot as fast as they could go, or rather, as fast as Pegasus could go. The old horse always tried to do his best for Sir Gadabout, but all this excitement wasn't really his cup of tea, and besides, his lumbago was playing up again.

When Camelot finally came into view, Herbert spoke. "Pardon me, sire," he said, "but perhaps you had better not go into the castle. Who knows what Rufus Redhead has been up to, especially if he's still disguised as you?"

"Of course," said Sir Gadabout. "I was just waiting to see if you would think of it yourself!"

So Herbert and Sidney Smith rode into Camelot while Sir Gadabout hid outside. After Herbert had taken care of his pony, they sauntered as casually as they could in the direction of Sir Gadabout's room to see what awaited them. On the way, they were stopped by Queen Guinevere, who was going to get a new bubble for her spirit-level.

"Is Sir Gadabout feeling quite well today?" she enquired.

Herbert and Sidney Smith exchanged nervous glances. "Er . . . I'm not really sure, your Majesty," Herbert answered edgily.

"Only I met him earlier on, and he had forgotten the way to his room; he seemed to

think I was the castle caretaker, and reported a bit of loose brickwork to me."

Herbert and Sidney made their excuses and put on a spurt to Sir Gadabout's room.

"You knock on the door," said Herbert through clenched teeth, "and when he opens it, I'll bop him on the nose."

"That'll solve all our problems," said Sidney Smith sarcastically.

Before they had gone another ten paces, they came upon King Arthur accompanied by

a detachment of armed guards.

"Have you seen Sir Gadabout?" he asked angrily.

"Er, not recently," replied Herbert.

"I've just had a serious report that he has run amok in the kitchens shouting something about 'halibut'. I'm afraid he's gone too far this time."

"He's just . . . ummm . . . sleepwalking, your Majesty," said Herbert loyally.

"*Sleepwalking*, at this time of day?" said King Arthur.

"I'd be surprised if anyone could tell the difference," commented Sidney Smith unhelpfully, and he and Herbert hurried off before they had to face any more awkward questions.

The door to Sir Gadabout's room was ajar, and as they approached, they could hear all manner of bumping, banging and cursing coming from inside. They peeped through the gap. Inside, Rufus Redhead, still in his Sir Gadabout disguise, was rummaging through drawers, opening cupboards, throwing things about, and shouting things like, "*I must have that turbot!*" and "*Where in Heaven's name has the oaf hidden the stickleback?*" Wigs, false noses and a variety of hats fell from his pockets as he charged around the room.

The sight was more than Herbert could bear. "Right!" he muttered darkly, forming his two big hands into two big fists. But Sidney Smith restrained him and, to his surprise, started talking in a loud voice.

"Excuse me, I'm a visitor here – I've come especially to see Sir Gadabout's collection of tinned fish . . ." The commotion inside the room ceased instantly. "Might I take a quick look?" Sidney Smith winked at Herbert and shook his head.

"Er, no," replied Herbert, cottoning on.

"Oh dear," continued the cat. "Then it's

true that King Arthur and Queen Guinevere keep the keys and won't let anyone into the room?" This time he nodded for Herbert's benefit.

"Yes, that's right . . ."

"But, if I did happen to get permission, I would have to go out of the main doors, turn left, and go into the East Tower, where I would see the appropriate sign?"

Watching Sidney Smith's nod, Herbert replied, "Yes."

The cunning cat ushered the squire outside.

"But," said Herbert, "that's the Round Table room . . ."

"Quick!" said Sidney Smith. "We need pen and paper."

Within minutes, Sidney Smith had produced a large square notice:

> **KEEP OUT**
> Sir Gadabout's Valuable Collection
> of Rare Tinned Fish

"This is Sir Henry Hirsute's fight," explained Sidney Smith. "We'll let *him* finish it." They made their way to the Round Table room, where Sidney Smith told Herbert to pin their notice to the door.

"Do you think it will work? He'll have a job getting in *there*."

"Rufus Redhead can get in anywhere, unless I'm very much mistaken," said Sidney Smith. "It's our job to make sure he can't get *out* again until . . . well, we shall see."

"Should we warn the King and Queen?" asked Herbert.

"Too risky," Sidney Smith replied. "They might give the game away or, worse, refuse to go along with my brilliant plan."

7

Guinevere's Right-Hook

Sir Gadabout – the real Sir Gadabout – couldn't wait any longer. His reputation – his *life* – was at stake. He set off in search of his companions.

The first person he met was Queen Guinevere. She was carrying a large key, and Sir Gadabout thought she might be feeling unwell, because she did not look quite as radiant as usual, and her eyebrows had turned red . . .

"Your Majesty," said Sir Gadabout, bowing politely. Queen Guinevere responded by biffing her knight on the chin, knocking him senseless – or, rather, more senseless than usual.

When he came to, some time later, Queen Guinevere was standing over him. She was carrying her spirit-level with its new bubble. "Very good right-hook, your Majesty," said Sir Gadabout tactfully. "But have I offended

Your Royal Highness?"

"What the dickens is going on?" asked the Queen, who now looked more like her old self.

"A very good question, your Majesty," agreed Sir Gadabout.

"First you cause pandemonium in the kitchens, then, a few minutes ago, I saw you jump out off a first-floor window straight on to the King and run away with one of his keys."

"Oh dear," groaned Sir Gadabout, realis-

ing the terrible truth. "Is that why you punched me?"

"Punched you? *Me?*"

Then Sir Gadabout did his best to explain about Rufus Redhead: how he had used a "Sir Gadabout" disguise to get into Camelot, but had probably donned a "Guinevere" disguise temporarily when he had seen the real Sir Gadabout coming. He wasn't very good at explaining complicated things, and it took rather a long time. But it ended with the Queen viewing him suspiciously. "But how do I know you are the real Sir Gadabout?"

He felt his aching jaw. "With respect, how do I know you are the real Queen Guinevere?"

They pondered this for a moment, till Guinevere suddenly raised her spirit-level like a sword. "Defend yourself!" she cried.

"Your Majesty . . ." stammered Sir Gadabout, horrified. But she insisted. He drew his sword, which was broken in the middle and held together with sticky tape. As soon as he held it aloft, the top half of the sword broke free from the sticky tape and disappeared down his sleeve. It made its way perilously

through his *Y-Worry?* Y-fronts, down his leg, and stabbed him in the foot. "Oooh! Argh! Eeeek!" he bellowed, hopping in a circle around the Queen.

"You're Gads, all right," remarked Guinevere.

"How," asked Sir Gadabout when he had sufficiently recovered, "would your Majesty fix a squeaking door?"

"Ah! Well, most people would just bung a bit of oil on the hinges, but that might clear the symptom without tackling the real cause of the problem. Personally, I'd remove the door completely after checking the way it

hangs, then I'd get a plane – a fine box plane, not one of those –"

"You are without doubt Queen Guinevere," said Sir Gadabout. "But if I'm not Rufus Redhead and neither are you, where is he and what is he up to?"

"He's heading for the Round Table room, sire," called Herbert, arriving on the scene with Sidney Smith. It appeared that Rufus Redhead was back in his Sir Gadabout disguise – as the owner of the tinned fish. Herbert explained Sidney Smith's plan, and added, "It won't be long before it's dark – Sir Henry Hirsute should take care of him."

"Not if Sir Henry thinks he's me," said Sir Gadabout. "The ghost is quite friendly really, and it will all have been a waste – a very painful waste – of time."

"The Keeper of the Privy Keys has another key," said Guinevere. "We'll get it and make sure nobody gets in or out of that room till daybreak, but first you must go in to ensure that Rufus's Sir Gadabout disguise doesn't fool Sir Henry."

Sir Gadabout gulped and turned pale. "What if the ghost gets us mixed up?"

"You'll soon find out," smirked Sidney Smith.

8
Sir Henry's Revenge

By the time the four of them arrived at the door to the Round Table room, it was already dark. Guinevere carried a candle to light the way. Standing behind the door, they could hear the same scuffling and bad-tempered grumbling which had earlier emerged from Sir Gadabout's room. Sir Gadabout silently opened the door and slipped inside. He heard the key turn in the lock behind him.

Rufus had his own candle, and was stomping around the vast room impatiently seeking the objects of his desire, and still wearing his Sir Gadabout disguise. He was so preoccupied with his search that he didn't notice Sir Gadabout, and Sir Gadabout decided, for the moment, to stay away from him and wait to see what happened.

After quite some time, when Rufus had searched the Round Table room from top to bottom and found nothing, he became angrier and angrier.

"WHERE IS THE FISH? I MUST HAVE THE FISH!" he roared.

"Patience, my friend," said an eerie voice which sent a shiver down Sir Gadabout's spine. Sir Henry Hirsute appeared from nowhere and walked towards Rufus. This time he looked quite human.

"Who – who are you? How did you get in here?"

"I am in charge of the collection of rare tinned fish," replied Sir Henry calmly. Sir Gadabout wondered how Sir Henry knew about the fishy story. He must be able to read minds! Sir Gadabout concentrated hard on thinking only good things about the ghost – just in case . . .

"Bah!" said Rufus. "There is no rare tinned fish in here – I've searched everywhere."

"You forget that this is Camelot," replied the ghost, "where the wizard Merlin has been known to work his magic. The rare tinned fish are protected by his spell, and are invisible to anyone who is deceitful – such as someone who tells lies, or *pretends to be someone else*." Sir Henry's voice sounded rather menacing, and Sir Gadabout wanted to make it quite clear that *he* was the real Sir Gadabout and not an imposter. But he didn't have time.

"I think I've seen you before . . ." said
Rufus.

"Yes, you have . . . but it was a long time
ago – about ten years, in fact." Sir Henry's
pale skin began to turn an angry red as he
recalled the torment he had been through
since Rufus Redhead had got him into all that

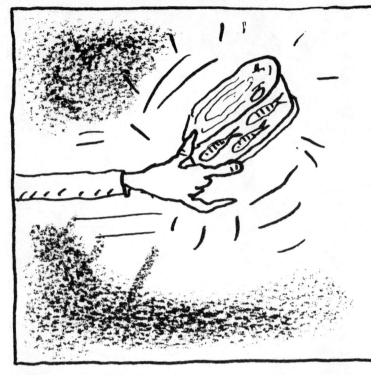

trouble. Sir Gadabout grew quite alarmed thinking about what Sir Henry might be capable of.

But instead, Sir Henry produced a tin of Cornish Stickleback out of thin air and held it out to Rufus; it looked quite real. "You may have this if you confess one of your worst crimes, such as pretending to be someone else . . ."

Rufus's eyes nearly popped out of his head when he saw the tin, which was a treasure

beyond his wildest dreams. "Er . . . er . . . I once disguised myself as a pair of kitchen scales in order to steal a tin of gudgeon," he admitted, snatching at the tin in Sir Henry's hand. It vanished.

"Oh dear," said the ghost. "It seems that you need to think back a little further than that. Try to remember something that got someone into a *great deal* of trouble." A large tin of Flying Fish from the Bay of Biscay appeared in the ghost's hand.

Rufus Redhead began to drool, and edged nearer, his hand twitching. "I impersonated a Health and Safety official in order to get a tin of Siamese Catfish," he confessed, making a lunge for the tin in Sir Henry's hand – but it had already disappeared.

Sir Henry Hirsute was now glowing scarlet with anger and impatience. Sir Gadabout felt certain that something terrible was about to happen. His knees gave way and he had to sit on the floor.

"Try to think back ten years!" The ghost roared so loudly that Rufus's candle blew out, but Sir Henry was now his true ghostly self, glowing so fiercely that it was no longer needed. "Confess! What happened here ten years ago? In these very kitchens?"

"I – I didn't do anything! It was a knight called Sir Hen –"

At that moment the ghost hovered closer to Rufus so that he could see him clearly.

Rufus's eyes grew as wide as saucers, and

his red hair stood on end. "You!" he cried, "You're Sir Henry Hirsute . . . but that's impossible!"

"Confess!" bellowed Sir Henry, and with a whoosh! he passed right through Rufus's body. The crook let out a blood-curdling yell. The colour drained dramatically from his hair, leaving it completely white while his face turned red.

Sir Henry turned and seemed about to pass through Rufus again. The master of disguise screamed, ran to the door and began pounding on it, crying, "It was me! Let me out! I stole the pilchards, not Sir Henry!"

Before the door could be opened, Sir Gadabout was also throwing himself against it, such was his terror. "It was *me*! I confess! Let me out!" he wailed pitifully.

After the chaos had subsided, the two Sir Gadabouts were hauled out of the Round Table room, quivering and burbling and each vigorously and earnestly insisting that he had stolen the pilchards, and would they please save him from the terrible ghost.

Rufus Redhead was in such a state that not only did he repeat his confession about what had happened ten years ago, but he announced that he would go home immediately and donate his entire collection of

tinned fish to the Hope's End Cats' Protection
League.

Queen Guinevere gave Sir Gadabout a big
hug and a kiss on the cheek for all his troubles,
which immediately made him feel miles
better.

A few days later, there was a ceremony in
the Round Table room at which a plaque was
unveiled in memory of the great and defi-
nitely honest Sir Henry Hirsute, who gave his
life for the honour of the Round Table. His

ghost was never seen again, and all-night sessions became the norm in the Round Table room. At the ceremony, Sidney Smith modestly told everyone how the whole plan had been his idea, and Herbert explained that the entire success of the scheme revolved around the authentic notice he had written and stuck on the Round Table room door. "I only learned to write three weeks ago," he admitted, "but you'd never have guessed."

Sir Gadabout explained that it was his

courageous yet sympathetic way of dealing with the ghost of Sir Henry Hirsute which had saved the day. Some said that was just a red herring, but before Sir Gadabout's words had died away, they heard ghostly laughter echoing in the corridors. And even though they knew deep down that Sir Gadabout was *still* the Worst Knight in the World, it was a long, long time before they mentioned it again.